IRON MAN ™
ARMORED ADVENTURES

DEADLY DREADKNIGHTS!

Adapted by Frank Berrios

Based on the original teleplay "Ancient History 101" by Alexx Van Dyne

Illustrated by Michael Borkowski

A Random House PICTUREBACK® Book

Random House 🏠 New York

Library of Congress Control Number: 2009943125

ISBN: 978-0-375-86141-3

www.randomhouse.com/kids

Printed in the United States of America

10 9 8 7 6 5 4 3 2

P9-BZS-072

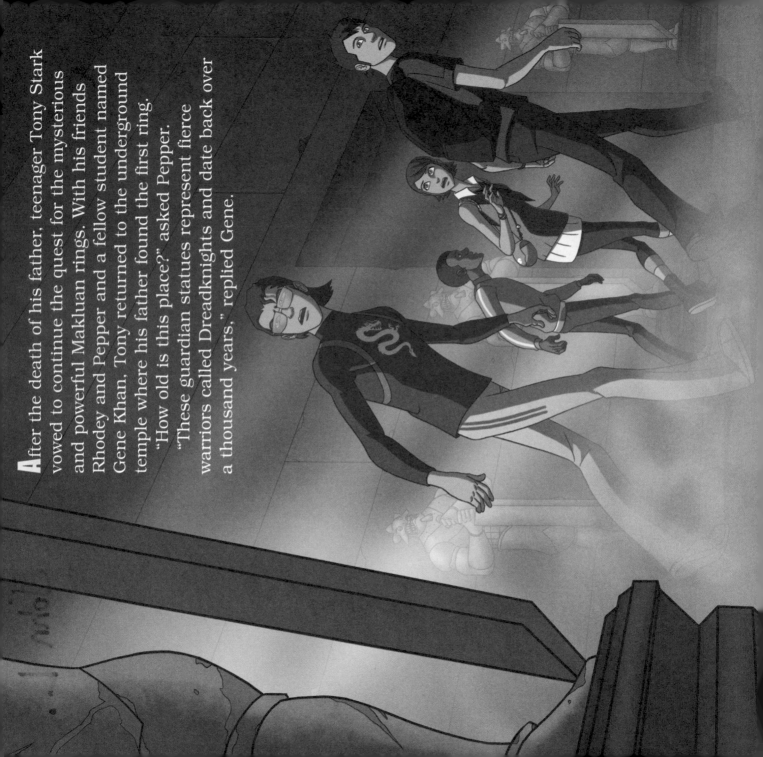

After the death of his father, teenager Tony Stark vowed to continue the quest for the mysterious and powerful Makluan rings. With his friends Rhodey and Pepper and a fellow student named Gene Khan, Tony returned to the underground temple where his father found the first ring.

"How old is this place?" asked Pepper.

"These guardian statues represent fierce warriors called Dreadknights and date back over a thousand years," replied Gene.

Huge, scary statues filled the temple, surrounding two stone pedestals. One pedestal held a book and the other a sword.

"My dad's diary mentioned tests," said Tony. "What if this is some kind of test? What if you have to choose one of these things to get to the ring?"

"Then it's not a very difficult test," replied Gene. "Wisdom equals book. Obvious."

"Begin," Gene said, reading aloud from the book. Suddenly, the temple shook! The floor began to crack and crumble away.

Tony and Pepper fell through the floor with the book and the sword just as Gene and Rhodey dropped into another dark chamber.

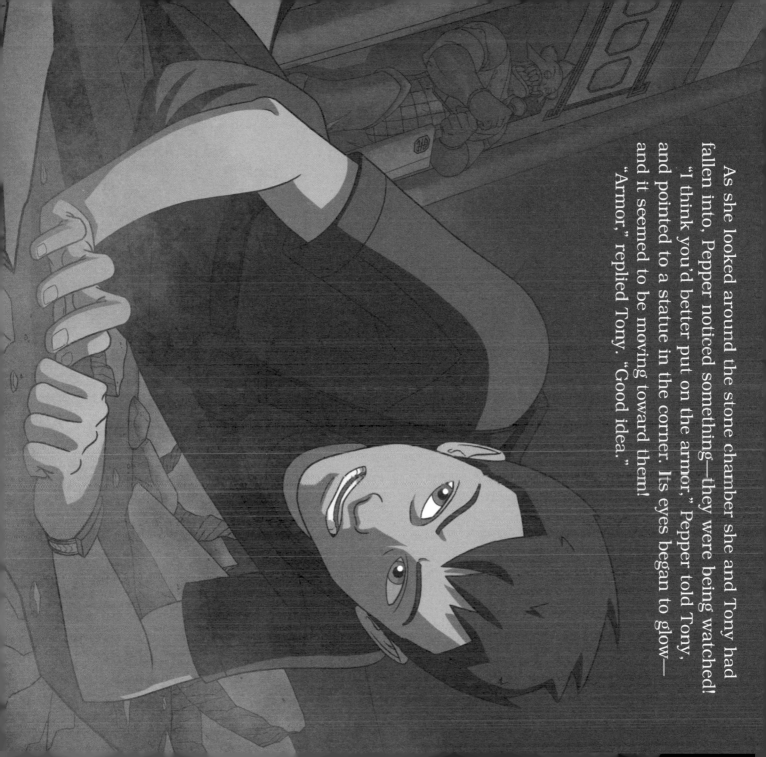

As she looked around the stone chamber she and Tony had fallen into, Pepper noticed something—they were being watched! "I think you'd better put on the armor," Pepper told Tony, and pointed to a statue in the corner. Its eyes began to glow— and it seemed to be moving toward them!

"Armor," replied Tony. "Good idea."

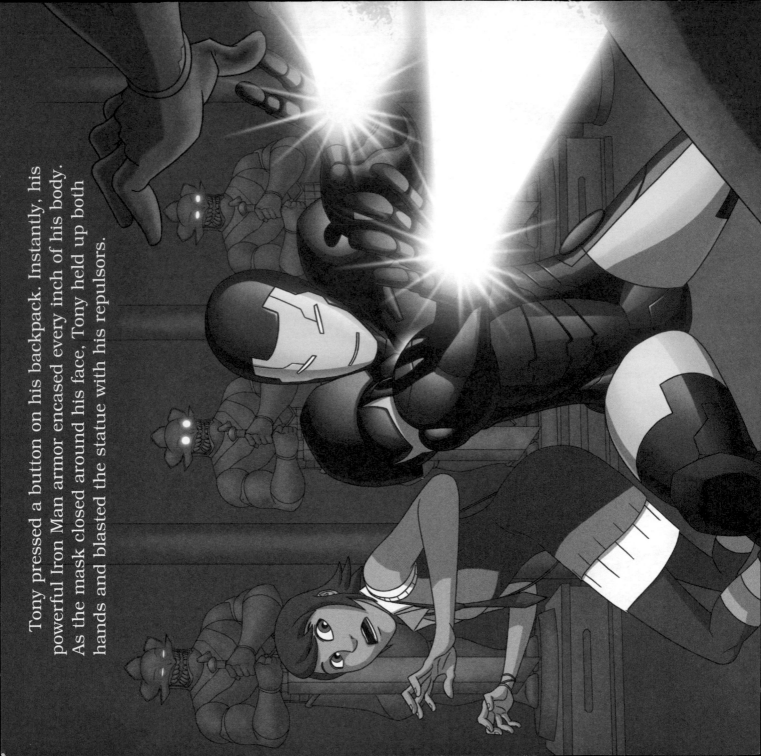

Tony pressed a button on his backpack. Instantly, his powerful Iron Man armor encased every inch of his body. As the mask closed around his face, Tony held up both hands and blasted the statue with his repulsors.

Meanwhile, Rhodey lay unconscious in another chamber. Gene removed the Makluan rings from his hidden necklace—and transformed into the villain known as the Mandarin! Tony and his friends had no idea about Gene's secret identity. As the Mandarin, Gene had already stolen two Makluan rings, and he was determined to get the others, to become more powerful.

"Kneel before your master," the Mandarin commanded the statues. Instead, they attacked! As he fought them, he said to himself, "So *this* is the test."

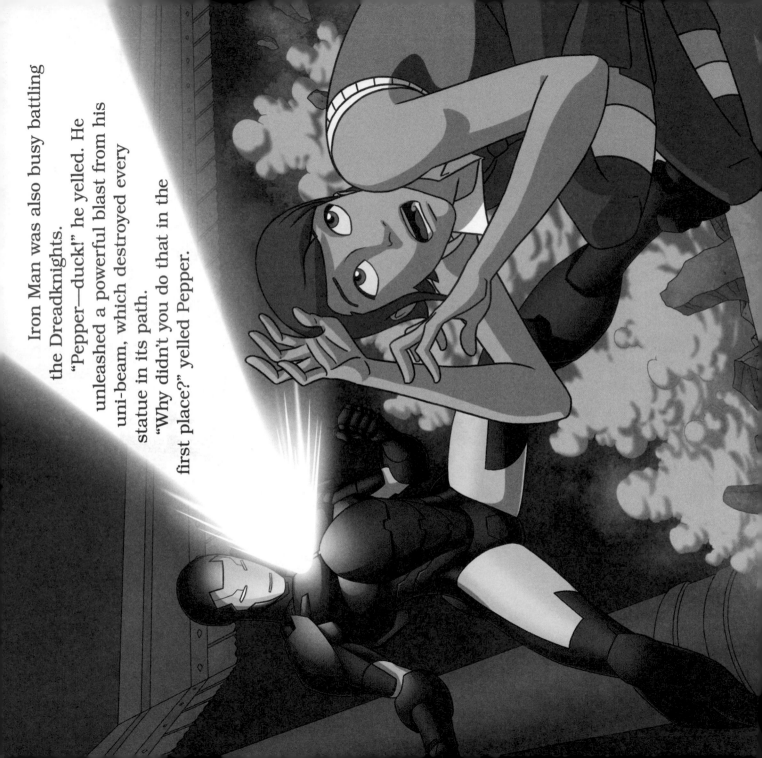

Iron Man was also busy battling the Dreadknights.

"Pepper—duck!" he yelled. He unleashed a powerful blast from his uni-beam, which destroyed every statue in its path.

"Why didn't you do that in the first place?" yelled Pepper.

More statues emerged from the walls. "Call me crazy, but I'm starting to think that fighting might not be the way to go here," Iron Man said.

"Well, surrendering seems like a mistake," replied Pepper. She picked up the sword that had been on the pedestal.

Iron Man spotted the book on the floor. "Gene read from this book and everything started to go bad," said Iron Man. "Maybe we can use the book to stop it, too."

Suddenly, Iron Man noticed something carved into the sword. "That symbol... that's it!" exclaimed Iron Man. "It's not the book, it's the sword that will end the test!"

"Computer, translate the glyph on the sword and give me the pronunciation!" said Iron Man as he battled a horde of Dreadknights.

"Glyph translated: 'end.' Pronunciation: *zwhong*,'" replied the armor's computer.

"Zwhong! Zwhong!" yelled Iron Man. The statues slowed to a stop—and crumbled to pieces right in front of him and Pepper!

Iron Man grabbed Pepper and rocketed out of the temple. When they were safely outside, Tony deactivated his armor and it folded up into his backpack.

Before Tony could go back to search for Rhodey and Gene, the temple began to collapse!

"No! Rhodey!" cried Tony as he raced to the edge of the crevasse—where he was surprised to see Gene and Rhodey alive!

Tony explained that the book had set the test in motion, but the sword had been the key to ending it.

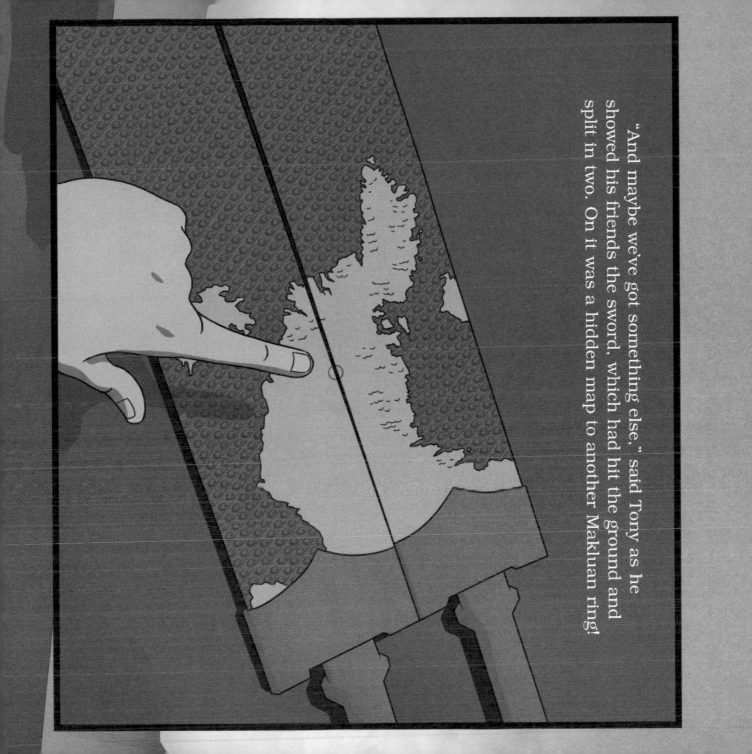

"And maybe we've got something else," said Tony as he showed his friends the sword, which had hit the ground and split in two. On it was a hidden map to another Makluan ring!

Tony knew he would find the Makluan rings one day. For now, he was glad that he and his friends had survived.

What Tony didn't know was that Gene would be waiting to use the rings for his own evil purpose—as the deadly Mandarin. . . .